Margaret Hillert's

Who Goes to School?

A Beginning-to-Read Book

Illustrated by Viki Woodworth

DEAR CAREGIVER,

The books in this Beginning-to-Read collection may look somewhat familiar in that the original versions could have been a part of your own early reading experiences. These carefully written texts feature common sight words to provide your child multiple exposures to the words appearing most frequently in written text. These new versions have been updated and the engaging illustrations are highly appealing to a contemporary audience of young readers.

Begin by reading the story to your child, followed by letting him or her read familiar words and soon your child will be able to read the story independently. At each step of the way, be sure to praise your reader's efforts to build his or her confidence as an independent reader. Discuss the pictures and encourage your child to make connections between the story and his or her own life. At the end of the story, you will find reading activities and a word list that will help your child practice and strengthen beginning reading skills. These activities, along with the comprehension questions are aligned to current standards, so reading efforts at home will directly support the instructional goals in the classroom.

Above all, the most important part of the reading experience is to have fun and enjoy it!

Shannon Cannon

Shannon Cannon,
Literacy Consultant

Norwood House Press • www.norwoodhousepress.com
Beginning-to-Read™ is a registered trademark of Norwood House Press.
Illustration and cover design copyright ©2017 by Norwood House Press. All Rights Reserved.

Authorized adapted reprint from the U.S. English language edition, entitled Who Goes to School? by Margaret Hillert. Copyright © 2017 Margaret Hillert. Reprinted with permission. All rights reserved. Pearson and Who Goes to School? are trademarks, in the US and/or other countries, of Pearson Education, Inc. or its affiliates. This publication is protected by copyright, and prior permission to re-use in any way in any format is required by both Norwood House Press and Pearson Education. This book is authorized in the United States for use in schools and public libraries.

Designer: Lindaanne Donohoe
Editorial Production: Lisa Walsh

LIBRARY OF CONGRESS CATALOGING-IN-PUBLICATION DATA
   Names: Hillert, Margaret, author. | Woodworth, Viki, illustrator.
   Title: Who goes to school? / by Margaret Hillert ; illustrated by Viki
     Woodworth.
   Description: Chicago, IL : Norwood House Press, [2016] | Series: A
     Beginning-to-Read book | Originally published in 1981 by Follett
     Publishing Company. | Summary: Simple text and illustrations depict
     animals in various work and training situations and concludes that school
     can be fun for animals and children.
   Identifiers: LCCN 2016001850 (print) | LCCN 2016022131 (ebook) | ISBN
     9781599538082 (library edition : alk. paper) | ISBN 9781603579704 (eBook)
   Subjects: | CYAC: Animals--Training--Fiction. | Working animals--Fiction. |
     Schools--Fiction.
   Classification: LCC PZ7.H558 Wh 2016 (print) | LCC PZ7.H558 (ebook) | DDC
     [E]--dc23
   LC record available at https://lccn.loc.gov/2016001850

288N—072016
Manufactured in the United States of America in North Mankato, Minnesota.

Who goes to school?
Can you guess?
No, no.
You can not guess,
but you will see.

Look here.
Look at this.
This is a school.
A school for dogs.

The dog will sit.
The dog will walk.
The dog will go with you.
This is good.

Here is a school, too.
And here are big dogs.
See what the big dogs do.

This dog gets into a car.
This dog will work.
He will work with the man.

Here is a good dog.
See this dog work.
He is a big help.

The dog will go out.
He will look and look.
He will find someone.

See this dog.
What can he do?
What is he good for?

This dog can work.
He can do good work.
He can help the man who
can not see.

And look at this little one.
What can she do?
Oh, look at this.

She did it!
She did it!
She is good.
What fun this is.

Here is a big baby.
It can do something, too.

It can sit up.

And here are big cats.
Big, big cats.

Cats at school.

The big cats sit.
The big cats play.
We like to see this.

Little cats go to school, too.
Look at this cat.
What a pretty one.

Now look at the TV.
Here is the little cat.
See what work she can do.
She is on TV.

This cat gets something.

She gets something little.
She is a big help.

This cat helps, too.
The man likes the cat.
What a good little cat.

Here is a school.
Boys and girls go to this school.

Do you go to school, too?

Yes, you do.
You read.
You work.
You play, too.

You have fun here.
It is fun to go to school.

Foundational Skills

In addition to reading the numerous high-frequency words in the text, this book also supports the development of foundational skills.

Phonological Awareness: The /w/ Sound

Sound Substitution: Say the words on the left to your child. Ask your child to repeat the word, changing the first sound to /**w**/:

talk = walk	me = we	pill = will	pay = way
mall = wall	cake = wake	save = wave	tag = wag
bear = wear	pin = win	dish = wish	poke = woke
nest = west	need = weed	paste = waste	bait = wait

Phonics: The letter Ww

1. Demonstrate how to form the letters **W** and **w** for your child.
2. Have your child practice writing **W** and **w** at least three times each.
3. Ask your child to point to the words in the book that start with the letter **w**.
4. Write down the following words and ask your child to circle the letter **w** in each word:

we	who	work	paw	with	cow	crawl
well	will	throw	what	walk	tower	low

Fluency: Echo Reading

1. Reread the story to your child at least two more times while your child tracks the print by running a finger under the words as they are read. Ask your child to read the words he or she knows with you.
2. Reread the story, stopping after each sentence or page to allow your child to read (echo) what you have read. Repeat echo reading and let your child take the lead.

Language

The concepts, illustrations, and text help children develop language both explicitly and implicitly.

Vocabulary: Animal Sounds

1. Write the following words on separate pieces of sticky note paper:

cat	dog	lion	bee	duck	bird	donkey
sheep	owl	chirp	roar	baa	hee haw	hoo
meow	quack	woof	buzz			

2. Read each word for your child.
3. Mix up the words and ask your child to match the animal names with the correct sound.
4. Mix up the words again and say each word randomly. Ask your child to point to the correct word as you say it.

Reading Literature and Informational Text

To support comprehension, ask your child the following questions. The answers either come directly from the text or require inferences and discussion.

Key Ideas and Detail

- Ask your child to retell the sequence of events in the story.
- What kind of animals went to school?

Craft and Structure

- Is this a book that tells a story or one that gives information? How do you know?
- Do you think the animals like going to school? How do you know?

Integration of Knowledge and Ideas

- Why do you think dogs can help people in the snow?
- If you had a pet, what would you train it to do?

WORD LIST

Who Goes to School? uses the 65 words listed below.

This list can be used to practice reading the words that appear in the text. You may wish to write the words on index cards and use them to help your child build automatic word recognition. Regular practice with these words will enhance your child's fluency in reading connected text.

a	find	into	play	up
and	for	is	pretty	
are	fun	it		walk
at			read	we
	gets	like (s)		what
baby	girls	little	school	who
big	go	look	see	will
boys	goes		she	with
but	good		sit	work
	guess		someone	
can		no	something	yes
car	have	not		you
cat (s)	he	now	the	
	help (s)		this	
did	here	oh	to	
do		on	too	
dog (s)		one	TV	
		out		

ABOUT THE AUTHOR Margaret Hillert has helped millions of children all over the world learn to read independently. She was a first grade teacher for 34 years and during that time started writing books that her students could both gain confidence in reading and enjoy. She wrote well over 100 books for children just learning to read. As a child, she enjoyed writing poetry and continued her poetic writings as an adult for both children and adults.

Photograph by Glenna Washburn

ABOUT THE ILLUSTRATOR Viki Woodworth is an artist and illustrator whose work has appeared in many books for children along with educational materials, magazines and activity books. Her fun, whimsical art style has entertained and charmed children for many years. She lives with her husband in the Midwest.